Best Brain of the Year

Story by

Precious Nwanganga

Written by

Ajumoke Nwaeze

© 2015

DISCLAIMER

This is a fictional story. Resemblance to any person or situation is purely coincidental.

DEDICATION

This story is dedicated to all learners who desire to become smarter.

ACKNOWLEDMENT

Cover Art & Illustrations by:

Dr Chris U. Mbah

krisgostev@yahoo.com

+2348105736730

It was the End of Year Prize Giving Day in Community Primary School Araba. The assembly hall was filled with Pupils dressed in their sparkling white and lush blue uniforms.

The girls had blue berets to match their chequered skirts, while the boys wore blue bowties on their white shirts. Parents and siblings of the pupils were also present and were dressed in their most special outfits.

The event started with an opening speech by Mrs Takwa, the school Headmistress. Then performances of poem recitations, song presentations, cultural dance displays, and a stage play followed. It was done by pupils of Basic One, Two, Three and Four respectively.

The senior pupils presented a debate on the topic "Extracurricular Activities: More Beneficial than Homework".
Pupils of Basic Six proposed the motion while Basic Five opposed.

It was time for the Prizes to be given. Mrs Takwa climbed up the stage in the company of two Teachers.

The hall was dead quiet; the only sounds heard were the beating of anxious hearts and the ticking of a wall clock.

Everyone waited eagerly.

"It is the culture of this school to appreciate pupils who dedicate time to study and demonstrate academic excellence and hard work."

Mrs Takwa's voice resounded from a megaphone. "This year, we have added one more award to the long list on our slate. This award is to encourage pupils to play less and study more."

The silence was broken with applauds and cheering from the crowd as different Prize winners were called up the stage to receive their award of excellence and hard work.

The winners of the new awards were also called out from each class. Among the recipients was Alyn Koka, an eight-year-old pupil of Basic Five, who usually came last in his class.

Alyn was always present in class and paid attention to his teachers but played a lot and never read his books after school.

Mrs Takwa handed him a wooden trophy engraved with the title "Best Brain of the Year." The trophy was beautiful and everyone wondered why Alyn was given the award.

Mr and Mrs Koka joined their son and the Headmistress to take photographs. They were happy because their son won a prize, but they were sad because his award was a contradiction – a mere

contraption.

8

During the term that followed, Alyn became the mockery of his classmates: the girls laughed at him for getting a booby prize; the boys refused to play with him during break period, and after school he was left to walk home alone, while they threw stones at him.

Alyn had no friends anymore; no one wanted to play with him because they saw him as a dumbbell. Every day in class he cried and buried his head in a desk. He was very sad.

His classmates preferred to cluster around Kodjo, the class Captain. They fought themselves to sit next to Kodjo; they gave him extra pencils and shared their meals with him. Kodjo was very brainy and for two years topped the class in his

Examination Report Card. He also received a prestigious award of excellence on the previous Prize Giving Day. It was a golden trophy.

One day, Alyn went to meet Kodjo. He wanted to find out from him how to be smart and brilliant.

"Kodjo, what do you do to pass your tests and exams with flying colours?" Alyn asked.

"Simple! I take my studies serious," Kodjo replied.

"Is that all?" Alyn suspected there was more to Kodjo's success than he was telling. He was prepared to find out, since it seemed Kodjo was not willing to tell him.

It was four weeks to third term Examination. Alyn was sitting under a tree behind the school building.

He was crying – he had failed his class tests.

Suddenly, Alyn caught sight of Kodjo, standing by a corner of the building. Kodjo looked left and right, but did not notice Alyn. He sneaked out a transparent bottle from his pocket. He brought out a capsule from it, shoved it down his throat hastily and swallowed it without water.

That night Alyn could not sleep, he thought about what he had seen Kodjo do and was convinced that Kodjo's secret of being brilliant was the capsule.

For the next few days, Alyn saved his lunch money. On the fifth day, he stopped by a Pharmacy on his way back from school.

"Good afternoon Sir", he said to a man at the counter who sold medicines. "I want to buy that capsule."

"What capsule?" the Pharmacist asked. "Doesn't it have a name?"

"I don't know the name, but I know it is long and white. The capsule makes people brilliant".

"Are you sure?" the Pharmacist asked.

"Yes Sir, I saw my classmate taking the capsule, and he is very smart. I want to be like him, even smarter."

The Pharmacist paused and thought for a while.

"Oh, that capsule, I have it. Promise me you will tell no one about this," he said.

"I promise, I won't tell even myself," Alyn replied.

"Good. Take this capsule once a day, every day for thirty days, then come back and tell me the result."

He handed Alyn a transparent bottle containing thirty capsules.

"Thank you Sir" Alyn said, and offered the money he had saved.

"Keep your money. You can pay after the medication works."

The Pharmacist looked around and whispered,

"One more thing, if you want it to work properly, open your books immediately after taking the capsule and read for at least one hour."

"Thank you very much Sir."

Alyn hurried home in excitement. He was very happy because his days of failing would soon be over.

* * *

Every afternoon, Alyn secretly took his medication as prescribed by the Pharmacist.

He opened his books after taking each capsule and read a few pages. The first day he could only read for fifteen minutes and dozed off. The second day he read for thirty minutes and his eyes became weary. The third day he read for one hour before he closed the book.

Two weeks after, Basic six had a class test, and Alyn got three answers right out of ten. His classmates were surprised. His Teacher was pleased with this improvement, and encouraged him to do better.

Alyn knew that the capsules were working, so he continued to take them and follow the instructions of the Pharmacist. He read his story books, he studied Mathematics, and he read Social Studies text books. He also studied Basic Science and did all his homework as well. He also played less and watched TV only on Saturdays.

The examination was in one week and Alyn still had fifteen capsules left. He wanted to finish the medication before his exams in order to have very sharp brains, so he doubled the dosage.

He took two capsules a day, one in the afternoon, and one in the evening. He also read in the afternoon after lunch and in the evening before bedtime. He read his books for one hour, sometimes he read for two to three hours. He really wanted the medication to work.

* * *

It was another End of Year Prize Giving Day. The assembly hall was filled with Pupils, Teachers, Parents and other Invitees.

This year, the Superintendent of Education in the State, Mr Labe had been invited as a Special Guest of honour for the occasion.

After the usual Performance Presentations, Mrs Takwa mounted the stage to present Prizes to the pupils.

"Last year, we added an award to the school's list to encourage pupils to take their studies more seriously.

"This year we have also added a scholarship fund scheme to some selected awards."

The crowd hailed Mrs Takwa after her speech.
She then called up Mr Labe to help present the
special awards to the winners. Everyone clapped
and cheered the different Prize winners who
received Awards.

"The Best Brain of the Year for Basic Six
goes to..."

Mrs Takwa paused for effect, and looked at the
crowd.

Their eyes lit up in anticipation, they were eager to
hear the name of the winner.

". . . Alyn Koka" she announced.

Everyone jeered Alyn. He was embarrassed and
sad. He felt bad that the capsules did not work,

and that he would have to endure another year of taunting and mockery. His parents were sad too; their son had won another booby prize. Mr and Mrs Koka were not aware of the medication Alyn had been taking; if they knew they would be angry with him.

The Headmistress afterwards announced that Alyn was entitled to a one-year scholarship in secondary school, and she explained why.

"You see, this young boy is among the few pupils who rose from the bottom of his class to the top. This shows momentous improvement and commitment to his studies.

"I desire that every pupil in this school emulates his footsteps. Alyn Koka has indeed proven to the entire school authority that he deserves to be the Best Brain of the Year.

"This time we are honouring his hard work with a golden trophy and not the caricature he received last year."

Everyone applauded Alyn for his hard work and prestigious award! Mr and Mrs Koka were no longer sad, they were happy because they could now easily send their son to Secondary School.

Alyn was very happy too! His happiness increased when his mother gave him a Thousand Naira note for making her proud.

Later that day, Alyn went to the Pharmacist to show his appreciation.

"Thank you very much Sir, the capsules really worked. I came first in my class and I won a scholarship." Alyn said in excitement.

"Whoa. I told you it would work, you can now pay me," the Pharmacist said.

Alyn handed him a thousand naira note and thanked him ceaselessly.

"I will come back next term and buy another bottle of capsules". Alyn said and left the Pharmacy.

All the while, a lady was standing behind, listening to the conversation.

She came forward to the counter and questioned the Pharmacist.

"Do you really think those capsules made him pass his exams?"

"Of course not, it was only a placebo, but he believes it made him brilliant - that's the placebo effect. I will tell him the truth the next time he comes," the Pharmacist replied smiling.

THE END

<u>Questions</u>

1. What is a Placebo?

2. Where did Alyn get the capsules from?

3. Who sold Alyn the capsules?

4. Did the capsules work?

5. What was the new Award added to the list of Awards?

6. Why did the Headmistress give Alyn the first award?

7. What was the true secret behind Kodjo's success?

8. Where did Alyn get money to pay for the capsules?

9. If you were Alyn's parents what would you do to the Pharmacist who sold capsules to your son without your knowledge?

10. What else did you learn from the story?

Glossary

Booby Prize: a prize given as a joke to a person who comes last in a competition or examination.

Brainy: Clever, brilliant, smart, intelligent.

Capsule: a small container with medicine inside which dissolves when swallowed.

Caricature: the art of making a drawing, painting or writing, of someone, which usually makes them look silly.

Contraption: any object.

Dumbbell: a stupid person.

Extracurricular: an activity or subject that is not part of the school usual course.

Medication: a medicine or a set of medicines or drugs used to improve a particular condition or illness.

Megaphone: a cone-shaped device which makes voice louder when spoken into, so people can hear from a far.

Mockery: a person or thing that is laughed at or mocked.

Momentous: Substantial, Significant, Important or Big.

Pharmacist: a person who is trained to prepare or sell medicines and who works in a hospital or medicine shop.

Pharmacy: a shop or part of a shop where medicines are prepared and sold.

Placebo: a substance given to someone who is told that it is a particular medicine, either to make them feel they are getting better or to satisfy them for not getting the thing they really wanted.

Scholarship: an amount of money given by a school or other organization to pay for the studies of a person with great ability but little money.

Taunting: an act of making fun of, or insulting someone into responding, often in an aggressive manner.

Trophy: a prize, such as a gold or silver cup, which is given to the winner of a competition or race, or to a person who comes first in anything.

About the Authors

Precious Nwanganga, (Pmoney) is a Sales & Marketing Professional, Entrepreneur, Blogger and Public Speaker. He writes fiction, non-fiction and creative non-fiction. As a young Writer, he emerged First runner-up in Cross River State Secondary School Poetry Competition, Junior Category, and since then has developed an intense fervour for creative writing.

He has published several articles on Business, Career, Politics as well as Fashion, Health and Social issues. Precious is the author of "*A Tale of Three Merchants*" and posts new articles from time to time on his blog and LinkedIn profile.

He blogs at www.pmoneytalks.com

Contact:

Twitter: @Pmoney_Talks

Email: hello@pmoneytalks.com

LinkedIn: https://linkedin.com/in/pmoneytalks

ClearVoice: http://clearvoice.com/CV/PreciousNwanganga

Ajumoke Nwaeze (AJ) is a Creative Artiste. She is a Singer, Writer, Blogger, Content Creator, and Public Speaker. The Port Harcourt born Gemini holds a Baccalaureate in Genetics/Biotechnology from University of Calabar, Nigeria. She writes short stories, fiction, and creative non-fiction, which reflect basic issues faced by an average youth.

Her work "**Lost in Brown Leaves**" was published in an anthology titled "**Songhai 12**" by Port-Harcourt World Book Capital. She is the author of "**The Pretty Teen**" and is working on other short stories; "**The Unpainted Taxi**", and "**A Night to Remember**" among others.

Ajumoke blogs at www.checkoutaj.com

Contact:

Instagram: @checkoutAJ

Twitter: @aj_ajumoke

Email: **ajumoke8@gmail.com**

www.ingramcontent.com/pod-product-compliance
Lightning Source LLC
Chambersburg PA
CBHW021409160726
47994CB00007B/3145

9 798580 400402